Whispers

of the Serpent

The Village Boy's Secret

Jaison Mayooran

ISBN: 1-912547-69-4
ISBN-13: 978-1-912547-69-2

This book is dedicated to
my friends and family.

This book belongs to:

_____

CONTENTS

Whispers

of the Serpent

The Village Boy's Secret

Jaison Mayooran

Chapter One

The Hidden Talent

In the small village of Shadowmere, nestled between the towering hills and lush forests, lived a boy named Jaison who extremely loved animals. He was like every other child in the entire village, helping his family with farm chores, playing by the river, and running through the open fields. But Jaison had a secret that no one else knew. A secret he had kept hidden for many years throughout his life.

Since he was little, Jaison had been able to hear the whispers of the serpent. It all started when he was playing in the woods one day, and he encountered a large, green snake. The snake, who seemed to shimmer in the scorching sunlight, had spoken to him in a voice as soft as the howling wind. At first, Jaison was terrified, but soon he realised that he could understand the snake's words and learn more about nature.

Over time, the creatures of the forest, snakes of all shapes and sizes, spoke to him sharing ancient knowledge and tales of the forest, and secrets no one else knew.

But Jaison had never told anyone his secret. He feared they would think him strange or, worse, a crazy village boy. Instead, he kept his gift hidden within his heart and lived a quiet life, often visiting the snakes when no one was around learning the knowledge that he never thought he could achieve.

Chapter Two

The Ancient Serpent

One day, as Jaison walked to the edge of the village to fetch a pail of water from the river, a great commotion filled the air. The villagers were in a frenzy, talking about a terrible disaster that was approaching the village. The crops had started to harden, animals had fallen ill, and there were whispers of an ancient curse that had awakened in the depths of the forest.

Curiously, Jaison slipped scraping himself on the moist soil into the woods to speak with the snakes. As he approached a large overwhelming oak tree, a serpent with dark red scales appeared before him. This was no ordinary serpent; it was Inferno, the ancient serpent, who had lived in the shadows of the forest for centuries.

"Jaison," Inferno hissed, his voice echoing in Jaison's mind. "The village faces a great danger. The curse is back, and it's connected to the missing Heartstone from the forest. Only one with the ability to speak to serpents can stop it."

Jaison's heart raced. He had heard stories of the Heartstone, a powerful gem said to protect the village from darkness. But no one knew where it was hidden, and no one had seen it for decades.

"You must find it, Jaison. You are the only one who can stop the village turning into darkness, here take a map this will lead you to the Heartstone," Inferno warned.

Chapter Three

The Journey Begins

Jaison knew he couldn't ignore the serpent's warning. He didn't fully understand his connection to the Heartstone, but he knew he had to try. He packed a small bag with food, water, and a few tools, and set off on an adventure into the heart of the forest.

Jaison followed his guts and took the map and sprinted through the forest jumping over thorns. Jaison ran as fast as he can feeling the courage that Inferno had gave him.

Jaison used that courage and pushed through all challenges until something bad approached him during the journey to find the Heartstone.

As he journeyed deeper into the forest, the air grew thick with mist, and the trees seemed to watch his every move. Jaison felt both excited and nervous he had never ventured so far into the woods before. But with the map there to guide him along the way, he felt a strange sense of courage.

Luckily, Jaison brought his gear and useful tools, so he had protection from the dangers that live within the forest. Jaison took his bag off and started to drink the energy juice he had with him so fast, that most of it just dribbled down his mouth onto the forest floor.

Chapter Four

The Shadowed Path

After several days of travel, Jaison arrived at a dark mystical place in one of the most dangerous places in the forest with poisonous frogs, jaguars and leopards. The trees here were deadly and ancient, their roots tangled in the earth like fingers clutching the ground. The air was thick with nothing but silence.

"Finally, the shadowed path, the first place on the map," Jaison muttered. The trees grew opening their eyes. "This place is dangerous, and you are the only one who could enter but most people who go in never return," whispered the tree in a croaky voice.

Jaison shivered. He could feel the weight of the forest pressing down on him. But he pressed on, determined to find the Heartstone to save his village.

As they walked, strange things began to happen. The shadows seemed to move, flickering and shifting like living creatures moving in the darkness. Jaison could hear whispers in the wind, soft, sinister voices urging him to turn back.

Jaison thought and remembered that his mum said there are ancient protectors that will try to lead you out of the forest and then eat you. Jaison ignored the voices of the ancient protectors.

Suddenly, the voice came back and said, "Your village will turn into dust if you don't turn back!"

But Jaison refused to turn back as he had come too far now. The only way was to keep on moving forward.

Chapter Five

The Enchanted Lake

After crossing the shadowed path, Jaison reached a sparkling lake. The water was crystal clear, and the surface shimmered with an otherworldly glow. In the centre of the lake stood a small island, where a gigantic snake slithered and slowly lifted its head about fifty feet off the ground. He spoke of course like all the other snakes did. "I will help you to cure your village from darkness as I am one of the three guardians of the village, my name is Swither, the power of water". The other two were Inferno, the power of fire and Ganash, the power of the Earth itself.

"I know Inferno," screamed Jaison in surprise.

"This is where the Heartstone was last seen," Swither said. "But be careful, Jaison. The lake is enchanted."

Suddenly, the surface of the lake rippled, and out from the depths rose a giant, serpentine creature, a water dragon. Its eyes glowed with a fierce, ancient light.

"Who dares disturb the waters of the Heartstone?" the dragon growled, its voice deep and thunderous. Swither slithered away and told Jaison to be careful because he is the king of the whole forest.

Jaison gulped.

"I am Jaison, from Shadowmere," Jaison said bravely. "I seek the Heartstone to save my village from darkness."

The dragon stared at him for a long moment before nodding. "You may pass, but only if you prove yourself worthy of seeing the Heartstone."

Chapter Six

The Trial Of The Heartstone

The dragon's voice echoed in the air as it disappeared back into the lake. A moment later, in the middle of the island something began to glow. A beam of light flashed through the forest as the beaming Heartstone rose slowly from the shimmering lake.

Jaison stepped forward, but as he did, the ground beneath him began to tremble. A wall of shadowy figures emerged from the forest, their eyes glowing red with hatred. They were the ancient protectors of the Heartstone, determined to stop Jaison from claiming it.

"You must face us, boy, if you wish to claim the Heartstone," one of the shadow figures said.

Jaison's heart pounded. He had never faced anything like this before. But then he remembered the serpents who had helped him so far. With a deep breath, he spoke to them.

"Swither, Inferno and Ganash! I need your help!" He called Ganash out even though he never even met him.

The serpents slithered to his side, including Ganash, he had black eyes with a hard rocky back. Their eyes were gleaming with determination. Together, they faced the shadowy figures, their combined strength and wisdom from the power that was gifted to all of them. With each hiss and strike, the serpents battled the protectors, while Jaison stood firm, his mind focused on the Heartstone ignoring everything in the background.

The protectors used their elements of fire, water and earth to attack the shadowy fingers, giving there all.

Chapter Seven

The Heartstone's Power

Finally, after what seemed like an eternity, the last of the shadowy figures was defeated in battle. Jaison reached out to put on his gloves and took the glowing Heartstone in his hands. The moment he did, a surge of energy flowed through him letting power emerge within him.

The Heartstone's power awakened something inside Jaison, an ancient magic that connected him to the very heart of the forest. He could feel the pulse of the land, the life force of every tree, every animal, and every serpent.

The Heartstone spoke to him in a voice like the wind through the leaves, "You have proven yourself worthy, Jaison. The curse will be lifted, but remember, with great power comes great responsibility."

Finally, Ganash, Swither and Inferno joined Jaison in the forest.

In surprise every one of the masters almost fainted as someone could witness the Heartstone power.

Then something clicked onto Jaison's mind, "If I have this power then one of my relative must have it too and they must be in my village".

Chapter Eight

The Return Of The Curse

With the Heartstone in hand, Jaison and the serpents made their way back to the village. But as they approached, they saw something terrible. The sky was darkening, and the village was surrounded by a thick fog. The curse had already begun to take its first step.

Monsters approached from every corner of the village and ghosts started to haunt people to death.

"We must hurry," Inferno hissed urgently. "The curse grows stronger with each passing second."

Jaison ran through the village, clutching the Heartstone tightly. As he reached the centre of the village, he held the stone high, calling on its power. The ground cracked, and the fog began to disappear. The Heartstone's light shone bright, and the curse slowly began to lift.

The ghost started to crackle in the sunlight while the monsters started to run in horror until they turned into smoke.

Chapter Nine

The Serpent's Blessing

With the curse lifted, the village was safe once again. The crops began to grow, the animals healed, and the villagers showed there smile once more. They praised Jaison for his bravery, but he remained humble, knowing that the real credit went to the three serpents who had guided him.

The serpents gathered around him, their eyes filled with pride. "You have saved the village, Jaison," Inferno said. "You are the true protector of the forest."

But Jaison knew he couldn't have done it alone. He had learned that sometimes, the most unexpected enemies could be the most powerful.

But friendship is one hundred times stronger and when family members believe in you, there is nothing you can't do.

Chapter Ten

The Village Boy And The Three Serpents

In the days that followed, Jaison's secret was safe. The villagers never knew the true story behind the curse's lifting, but Jaison often found himself walking through the woods, speaking to the serpents. Jaison had become one with the forest and humans connecting them both in harmony.

And every time he heard the soft whispers of the serpents, he smiled. He knew that he had a special secret with the creatures of the forest a secret that would never be broken.

The whispers of the serpent would always guide him, as they had guided him around the danger and to victory. And Jaison, the boy with the secret, was no longer just a village boy—he was the guardian of the forest, the protector of the Heartstone, and a friend to all sides of the forest creatures and all humans.

Couple of years later he crossed paths with the three heroes once again—but this time, the curse was unlike anything he had ever imagined. Nature itself was being destroyed, twisted, and corrupted, and the land was falling under a dark, invisible grip.

The whispers of a forgotten evil stirred in the air, and the heroes, once filled with confidence, now wore shadows of doubt on their faces. Something ancient, something far worse than before, was at work—and Jaison could feel it in his bones.

Can they protect the forest from danger?

Only time will tell.

SNAKES

Snakes are cold-blooded reptiles and carnivores, meaning they eat other animals. Because they are cold-blooded, their body temperature shifts based on the temperature of their surroundings.

Snakes can be found in many different habitats, such as forests, swamps, grasslands, deserts, and even in fresh or salt water. Some snakes are active dur the night, while others are active in the daytime. As predators, they feed on wide range of animals, including rodents, insects, bird eggs, and young birds.

WHAT DO THEY EAT?

Nearly all snakes swallow their food whole. Their jaws are flexible, allowing them to open their mouths very wide. Different snake species have different diets. Some eat mammals, birds, eggs, snails, fish, or even other snakes.

HOW DO THEY CATCH PREY?

It can take snakes anywhere from a few days to several weeks to fully digest their meal. Some species prefer to sneak up and ambush their prey, while others are more aggressive, relying on speed and strength to overpower their target.

WHAT DO THEY LOOK LIKE?

Snakes have long, slender bodies without any legs or arms. Most have sharp teeth, and some types even have large fangs. Their bodies are covered in scales. There are more than 3,000 species of snakes, and they come in a wide variety of colours and sizes. Snakes don't have eyelids, and they use their forked tongues to sense their surroundings.

Activities

AFTER READING

How much can you remember
about the story?
Take this quiz and find out!

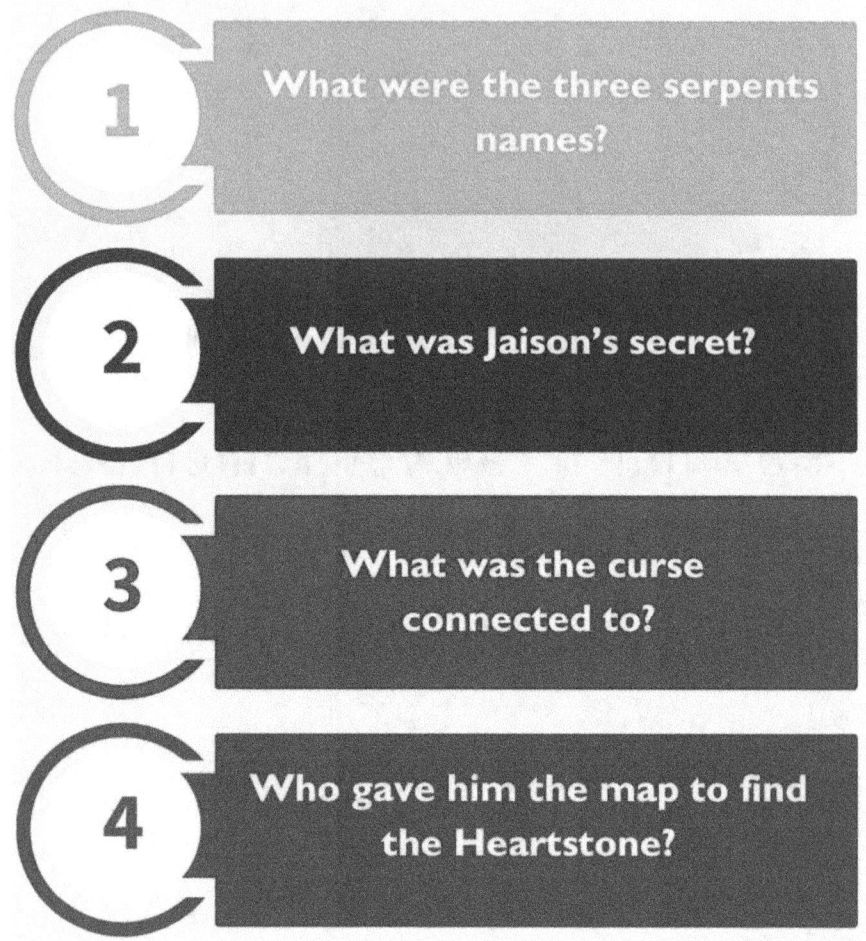

1. What were the three serpents names?

2. What was Jaison's secret?

3. What was the curse connected to?

4. Who gave him the map to find the Heartstone?

1. Inferno, Swither and Ganash
2. He can talk to snakes
3. The missing Heartstone
4. Inferno

Crossword

S	T	O	N	E	A	T	C
A	E	F	E	A	R	E	U
F	O	R	E	S	T	R	R
E	A	H	P	R	U	C	S
P	L	A	K	E	O	E	E
E	S	E	K	A	N	S	S
W	H	H	E	A	R	T	A
V	I	L	L	A	G	E	N

Find the following words:

STONE	HEART
VILLAGE	SNAKE
FEAR	FOREST
CURSE	SECRET
SAFE	SERPENT

Have fun colouring

MAZE GAME

Can you get Jaison to his
serpent friend the right way?

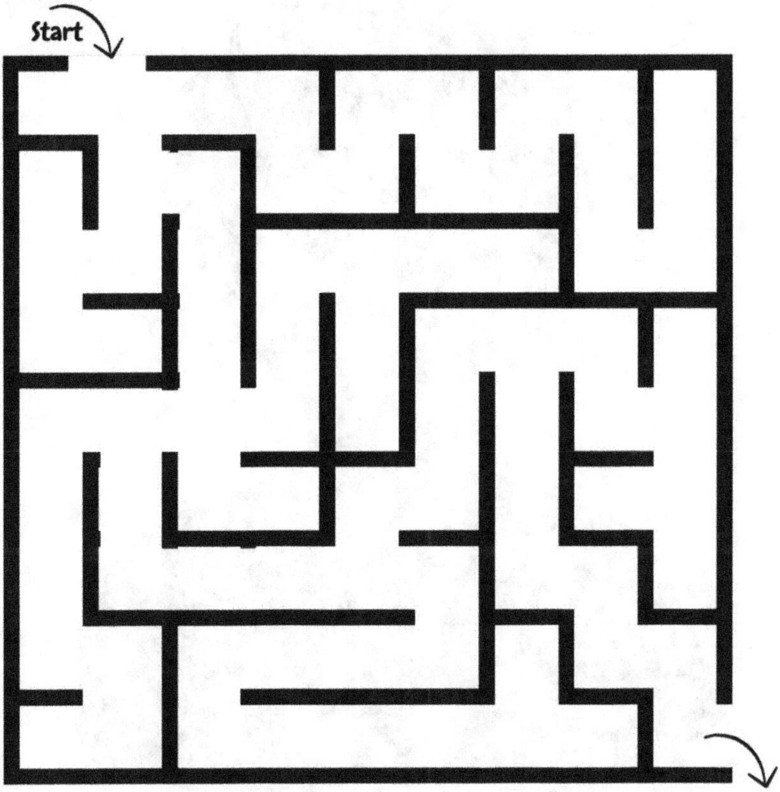

Start

About the Author

Meet Jaison, a curious and adventurous 9-year-old boy with a deep love for animals, especially snakes! From a young age, he has been fascinated by the wonders of nature, spending countless hours observing creatures big and small.

His passion for animals and the outdoors has inspired him to write this book, where he shares his love for the natural world in a fun and exciting way. When he's not reading about or studying animals, you can find him exploring the wilderness, learning about different species, and imagining the amazing adventures they might have.

With this book, Jaison hopes to inspire other young readers to appreciate and protect the world around them,
just as he does.

NOTES

NOTES

NOTES

NOTES

NOTES

NOTES